HOLY LOVE

CLAIRE ELIZABETH GROSE

DEDICATION

This book is dedicated to Jeanette and Peter
My beloved sister and brother-in-law

CONTENTS

DEDICATION IV

CONTENTS V

PREFACE VIII

ACKNOWLEDGEMENTS..X

PART ONE 1

    MY DAILY PRAYER 4

    A LOVE 5

    THE MAGNITUDE OF YOUR POWER............................. 6

    QUALITIES WITHIN 7

    MAKE WAY FOR THE SAVIOUR 8

    I LOVE YOU... 9

    MOMENTS OF VICTORY 10

    YOU ARE THE REASON 11

    WORDS OF LOVE 14

    PRECIOUS HOLY SPIRIT... 15

    MY SANCTUARY 16

    LOVE YOU CAN'T COMPARE...................................... 17

    TALK TO GOD 18

    LIVE BY THE HEART 19

    THE GREAT COMFORTER 20

    ONE IN YOUR LOVE 21

    ANYTIME PRAYER.. 22

    MY FORTRESS AND ROCK.. 23

    EMBELLISHED LOVE 26

    A LISTENING HEART 27

    A QUIET PLACE 28

    BE A LOVING VESSEL 29

PART TWO 30

    SHARE HIS LOVE TODAY.. 33

    DEPEND ON YOUR FAITH 34

    CHEER ME UP LORD 35

    FOLLOW HIS CALL 36

MY HEALER, MY HOPE 37

EMPOWER US 38

ARM OF TRUST 41

A CHILD OF CHRIST 42

THE PEACE OF GOD 43

JESUS, BE WITH ME 44

HEART MOODS 45

EMBRACE ME 46

HIGHS AND LOWS 49

THE DAY YOU CAME TO STAY 50

NOURISHMENT 51

TELL ME YOU LOVE ME 52

LOVING YOU 53

HEAL THE HURT 54

FLOW OF LIFE 57

INVIGORATE ME 58

SPIRIT TOUCH 59

COMMUNE WITH THE SAVIOUR 60

SURGE AHEAD 61

FULL CIRCLE 62

THE GREAT PROVIDER 63

THE HEART OF GOD 64

SOME DAYS 65

MY GUIDE 66

COMMUNE CLOSELY 67

FAITH BRINGS ETERNITY 68

PART THREE 69

FOREVER YOU WILL REIGN 72

YOUR LOVE DIVINE 73

ETERNAL SHEPHERD 74

ETERNAL TREASURE 75

BELIEVE TO RECEIVE 76

CONNECT AS ONE 77

HIS GIFT OF LOVE 80

SOLITUDE 81

WE ARE LOVED.. 82

I'M IN YOUR LOVING HANDS 83

PEACE AND CALM 84

NURTURE ME 85

PART FOUR 86

THE UPPER ROOM 89

MURMURS OF EASTER 90

BLESSED ONE, CHRIST JESUS... 91

I REJOICE 94

HE LIVES 95

A DIMLY LIT STABLE 98

IN THE SILENCE OF THE NIGHT....................................... 99

THE NEWBORN MESSIAH KING... 100

HOLY LOVE 101

PREFACE

Two things I just wanted to say about this book are, why I started writing and how I came by the title.

I grew up in the 1950's-1960's in Adelaide, South Australia, my life was pretty simple but wonderful. I was very lucky to have a secure family life, and my Mum and Dad brought the family up to treat others with respect, do the right thing, be courteous, and respect your elders. We had a strict upbringing and even as adults our parents never criticized us but encouraged us to do our best in life. They were "Aussie battlers" but we always managed to make it through the tough times!

They were people of integrity and cared about others and instilled that into our family.

Church was a big part of our lives growing up. We went to Sunday School at an early age and progressed up through the appropriate groups as we got older.

Youth groups, camps and church anniversaries were all important to the whole family. We competed in Church sports teams, basketball and tennis with other Parishes across Adelaide. Life-long friendships were in the making and cherished golden memories to look back on that would never fade.

Bible stories, hymns and choruses were all part of getting to know Jesus. This nurturing finally led me to the day Jesus came knocking on my heart's door. Being filled with the Holy Spirit is something I will never forget and the overwhelming power of His love that filled my whole being and propelled me to the front of the hall to give my heart to Him. No words can fully describe the joy I felt. That was in February 1968, I was 14 years of age. He has been my Shining Light ever since, and lives within me always.

So I thank my beautiful Mum and Dad for the way they raised me and for the foundation of knowing Jesus' love.

It was in His love that I started to write, in the autumn of 1993. My journey has brought me to this book "Holy Love", because God is Love!

"…God is love, and whoever lives in love lives in union with God and God lives in union with him." 1 John 4:16 Good News Bible.

God's love is such a powerful thing that I wanted to write poems reflecting His glorious love and how it can change our lives in a moment! Most of the poems in this book are about His love and my prayer is that He will speak to you, so you will know His love.

When I was a young Christian reading my Bible was really important to me in getting to know Jesus as my personal Saviour and became the foundation that I built my faith on.

It gave me strength and courage as I began life in the workforce at the age of 16. Coming from a sheltered upbringing it was my life-line to self-confidence and adapting to social life at work.
The poems reflect the everyday feelings and emotions that we feel as we meet the challenges of life and how the great magnitude of God's love can help us rise above them.

I pray you will turn to Him not only in your hour of need but in celebration of happy times in your everyday life. He longs to be your Saviour and confidante so you can share everything with Him, the Holy God Himself!

Many of these writings have been my first words of whispered prayer, so much that I have been moved to write them down at once and continue on in His wonderful and absolute love.

Together we write as He provides my inspiration.

All glory to Him, my precious Lord Jesus!

ACKNOWLEDGEMENTS

My heartfelt thanks to my beloved family, my Mum and Dad, Lilly and Ken, and my siblings Jeanette, June, Carol, Gloria and Lynne, for their never ending encouragement and support to me. To the rest of the family, you are all a precious link that joins us together.

To Michael and Andrew for your continual support to me in fulfilling my passion of writing poems for the Lord to help others through His Word.

A huge thank you to Junie for editing my poems and the coffees and lunches we enjoyed along the way.

To Joy Furnell for her Crown of Thorns drawing, you have an amazing gift, thank you Joy.

A big thank you to Jeanette, Pete, Carol, Den, Allan and Barry for photos.

To my friends and Church Families, thank you for your love and support.

To my beautiful sons, Michael and Andrew, thank you for loving me, and I am so glad He gave you to me. I will love you forever. To your partners and my grandchildren, I love you all so much.

To you the reader, thank you for picking this book up and I pray you will find His peace and love on the pages ahead.

May He shower you all with His love and blessings.

PART ONE

"love is patient and kind; it is not jealous or
conceited or proud; love is not ill-mannered or
selfish or irritable; love does not keep a record of
wrongs; love is not happy with evil, but is happy with
the truth. Love never gives up; and its faith, hope,
and patience never fail."

1 Corinthians 13 : 4 - 7

GOD IS LOVE…

"My commandment is this: love one
another, just as I love you."

John 15 : 12

MY DAILY PRAYER

Be with me, stay with me,
Close by my side,
Fill me with Your peace and love,
So my spirit shall surely fly
To the heights in Your love,
As only You can give,
Prepare me for this day ahead,
So in me You'll always live.

A LOVE

A love so great
Will never let you go,
A love that can change you
To pure as snow.

A love that demands
Your trust and belief,
A love so real
You will want to seek.

A love so powerful
You just can't hide,
His Words of truth
Will come from inside.

A love that brings
The Holy Spirit to you,
A love that makes you
Feel brand new!

A love so glorified
That Heaven's angels can see,
A love so bright
That changes you and me.

A love that will make you
Cry joyous rivers of tears,
A love from Eternity
Will bring God near!

THE MAGNITUDE OF YOUR POWER

For every crowning sunrise,
A day will unfold,
Your presence is still with us Lord
As in days of old.

In every bowing sunset
We see Your colours shine,
Such glory of Your power
That thrills this heart of mine.

Then the sprinkling of the stars,
Wonder slowly awakes,
The magnitude of Your power,
How You put them in their place.

Lord, You are in Your heaven
Where Your power abounds,
Love is everywhere
And Your glory is found.

QUALITIES WITHIN

No matter what's on the outside,
It's the inside that counts,
God measures our kindness
And thoughtfulness, no doubt!

He sees into each heart
And knows your abilities,
He's given His gifts to each one
To use abundantly.

It may take some time to discover
These qualities within,
But if you live by your heart
God's rewards He will bring.

No matter what's on the outside,
Keep your heart warm and safe
In the hands of the Saviour,
He will fill it with His grace.

MAKE WAY FOR THE SAVIOUR

Make way for the Saviour,
Give Him room in your heart,
He's the one who knows everything
That lies in your heart.

Make way for the Saviour,
His Holy Spirit will come to share
The Lord's love in all its fullness,
Your heart will feel Him there.

Pure joy you will know,
To your knees you will fall
And worship Him completely,
When you answer His call.

Make way for the Saviour,
The Blessed Holy One,
So you will know pure joy
From God's only Son.

Make way for the Saviour,
Allow His ways and Words
To overflow within you
Because you, He came to serve!

I LOVE YOU

I love You because You're here,
You're never far away,
Close by my side
You will always stay.

I love You because You're my protector,
Guiding and guarding each day,
You help me with the events of life
That come my way.

I love you because You're my counsellor
For all the challenges I face,
To You I surrender everything
As I state my case.

I love You because You're my Prince of Peace,
My King of Kings and my Lord,
Precious Holy Redeemer
To You I give my all.

MOMENTS OF VICTORY

Your heart will know pure love
When Jesus comes to live,
He is in your heart forever
When you give it to Him.

Others in His fold
Will take you in,
The same love you share
When you give your heart to Him.

You may not know them
But His love you share,
Moments of victory
Because in His love you care.

Moments of victory
Flood your mind and soul
Along life's journey
When you are one of His fold.

YOU ARE THE REASON

You are the reason Lord
For my happy heart,
Because of You
I have made a new start.

You gave me Your love
Many years ago,
Your Holy Spirit came to me
And blessed me so.

You are the reason Lord
I have the strength to climb,
Lifes ever changing landscape
That will dip and rise.

You are the reason Lord
I can face each day,
You are my guide and shield
Your light will never fade.

REFRESH US…
WITH EVERY NEW DAWN…

"Remind me each morning of your constant love,
for I put my trust in you…"

Psalm 143 : 8

WORDS OF LOVE

Words of love are Yours Lord
From Your home; Eternity,
Nothing can bind them down
From sin we can be free.

Your voice from Eternity
Is filled with pure love,
To every heart that opens
Is filled with Your Holy love.

Reach out for His touch
That spans the centuries,
Time makes no difference
To the one from Galilee.

His presence so demanding
Will hush the slightest sound,
His Words of love forever
To each precious heart are bound.

God's Words of love an anchor
That will give us stability,
Open your heart to Jesus
He loves you endlessly!

PRECIOUS HOLY SPIRIT

The soul moves in love
Where the Holy Spirit lives,
Moments of pure gold
To your heart He brings.

No words can explain
His pure love that flows,
Mountain top moments
You will surely know.

Thank Him for the way
He shows the Lord divine
In great magnitude,
To each bud on the vine.

He will nurture your precious soul,
The one true part of God,
Connected to His Spirit
Where His pure love unfolds.

MY SANCTUARY

Profound peace is around me
When I visit my sanctuary,
A place of calm and quiet,
Where the sea speaks to me.

My worries seem to leave me,
I let the tide take them away,
This is my sanctuary
Where my healing takes place.

There's nothing like a sea breeze
To refresh and settle the mind,
Thoughts are hushed and still,
Rest comes to this heart of mine.

My sanctuary I love,
Where I commune with God,
My life-buoy is around me,
The strength I can lean upon.

LOVE YOU CAN'T COMPARE

The Lord's love is so outstanding,
Nothing can compare,
Divine love in all its fullness
You will want to share.

The Saviour's love is forever
It will never change,
His power and His glory
Will always be the same.

Nothing will ever divide
His great love for you,
It is there for all time
No matter what you do.

All the gems in this earth
Could never outweigh
The Saviour's love for you:
Call the King of Kings today.

His love you can't compare
To anything in this life,
Open His Word to follow
The precious Lord Jesus Christ!

TALK TO GOD

Talk to God to know
Reassurance within your heart,
When you know Him as your Saviour,
Peace and calm He'll bring to your path.

Talk to God and thank Him
For His loyalty and grace,
Every day of your life
He knows what you will face.

Make room for the Saviour
Who loves you endlessly,
Connect with God today
So you can face reality.

Talk to God today,
Claim peace and calm inside,
His hand will be upon you,
He will always be your guide.

LIVE BY THE HEART

Live by the heart,
Lift your sight higher,
Rewards you will reap,
Make His will your desire.

The Saviour looks
At the heart inside,
Compassion and kindness
Is what He wants to find.

The Saviour is love
Which we feel in our heart,
His strength will feed you
If you will only ask.

Yes, live by the heart,
The Saviour tells us so,
For favour with God
Let your love show.

THE GREAT COMFORTER

The great Comforter; the Holy Spirit
Shows God's love to us,
Forever He will reign
Over all and what is to come.

The divine Holy Spirit,
The great Comforter Himself,
Jesus gave Him to us
To make His presence felt.

He brings Holy love
In great magnitude,
Gifts beyond understanding
Are waiting for you.

He brings God's love to comfort us
Through our daily walks,
When we commune with Him,
Our soul will rejoice!

ONE IN YOUR LOVE

When the Lord puts people on your path
Some shine like pure gold,
That's when He comes to bless you
Because they are in His fold.

We can share His mighty love,
We are in His family,
Shining in His light
We are nurtured by Thee.

Our faith is open wide
In His beauty and grace,
Sharing the same love
We see Your face.

Being one in Your love,
Such a precious gift,
I praise and worship You Lord,
Thank You for all You give.

ANYTIME PRAYER

How lucky am I
To talk to You Lord?
Anytime, anywhere
You hear my prayer.

How lucky am I
That You always care?
You carry each heart
From way up there.

How lucky am I
That I love You so?
You changed my heart
Many years ago.

Thank You precious Lord
For anytime prayer,
No matter where I am
You will be there.

MY FORTRESS AND ROCK

Thank You for loving me
And showing me Your ways,
My heart feels Your hand
On my lowest of days.

When I am happy
I have a spring in my step,
That's when You shine the brightest,
Your love pours from my pen.

On the testing days
When I need You the most,
My spirit is low and fragile,
I call You to come close.

Your love for me so strong;
A mighty fortress and rock,
Nothing can stand against You
Your love will never stop.

25

INVITE HIM INTO YOUR HEART…

"Seek your happiness in the Lord, and he
will give you your heart's desire."

Psalm 37 : 4

EMBELLISHED LOVE

The embellishment of Your love Lord
Beautifies the soul,
Sparkles in Your Spirit
He has made me whole.

A love so glorified
Fills me so,
From my precious Holy Saviour
Embellishment flows.

My soul restored
Because His love reveals
Magnified joy
That I cannot conceal.

Embellished love
Words cannot describe,
Continuing to flourish
In His love I just can't hide.

A LISTENING HEART

Thank You for Your love Lord,
That forever more will last,
Thank You for every listening heart
For Your will to come to pass.

Help us to be mindful
Of the needs You send to us,
Give us strength to deal
With the cares that we must cast.

Open each listening heart
To make room for Your work,
You know the future ahead
And the hands that will serve.

Help us to be brave
For every waking day,
To truly be Your witness,
For the hearts that must be saved.

A QUIET PLACE

When I'm quiet with You Lord,
My heart feels blest,
Peace comes to me,
In You I have rest.

In You I have a sanctuary,
Profound peace I find,
I ask for Your calm
To ease my troubled mind.

Every day I have to find
A quiet place with You,
Spiritual food I need,
To feed my faith in You.

Thank You Lord for Your peace
So profound in every way,
Finding a quiet place with You
Is joy that never fades.

BE A LOVING VESSEL

The Saviour's love will change
The heart and soul
Into loving vessels
That His hands will always hold.

The Saviour's light so bright,
Earthly eyes just cannot see,
Be a loving vessel
So His love you can receive.

Wonders wait before us
A reward to behold,
Joy beyond knowing
For each in His fold.

So be a loving vessel
Filled with God's love,
His kindness and compassion
You can pass on.

PART TWO

"And we ourselves know and believe the love which God has for us. God is love, and whoever lives in love lives in union with God and God lives in union with him."

1 John 4 : 16

THE WORLD MAY HURT ME…
BUT JESUS WILL HEAL ME…

"Be always humble, gentle, and patient. Show your love by being tolerant with one another."

Ephesians 4 : 2

SHARE HIS LOVE TODAY

Share His love today,
Happiness you will find,
You can show a little kindness,
Just open your heart wide.

Share His love today
To a world full of pain,
Hold out the hand of Christ
To bring hope and not dismay.

Share the love of God
In a smile or a kind word,
Encouragement goes a long way
When it is heard.

So show the love of Christ
To a weary heart,
Extend the hand of kindness
So that healing can start.

DEPEND ON YOUR FAITH

Walk through each day in His love,
No matter what you do,
If you're walking in His love
He will guide you through and through.

Rely on your trust,
Depend on your faith,
Each day with the Saviour
Is living in His grace.

You are His beloved
In each walk of life,
Everyone in this world
Can walk in His light.

Depend on your faith,
Live in His peace,
Rely on your trust,
His love will never cease.

CHEER ME UP LORD

Cheer me up Lord
When my heart feels low,
Lay Your precious hands on me
So Your Spirit flows.

Only You can lift me up
Away from my doubts,
Your grace and mercy
Makes me want to shout!

Some days my focus is short
And my patience low,
Almighty Heavenly Father
Touch me, so Your Spirit grows.

I need You every day Lord
To cheer me up,
In Your light I can feed
On Your glorious love.

FOLLOW HIS CALL

You owe it to your heart
To stay in a calm and happy place,
Seek His arms of pure love,
Seek His precious face.

Open your mind to His Word,
For He is love divine,
Listen for His prompts,
His strength is sublime.

His grace and mercy are there
For everyone to find,
Make compassion your goal,
Carry a heart that is kind.

Follow His call in your heart,
So His anointing can take place,
When you belong to the Saviour
You will receive His mercy and grace.

Claim Him as your counsellor
For peace and calm always,
Follow His call in your life,
Now His Spirit has come to stay.

MY HEALER, MY HOPE

Jesus, You are my healer
For every need I have,
Your anointing so precious
From You, the Son of Man.

Jesus, You are my hope
For every challenge of life,
You are my armour and shield
As I walk in Your light.

Jesus, You are my guide
Along the path I take,
You go before me
Whatever choice I make.

Jesus, You are my Master,
You show me how to live,
Forever in Your light,
My Father, Lord and King.

My healer and my hope
Into Eternity,
As Your child I will see
You on Your Throne in victory.

EMPOWER US

Empower us Lord
With Your anointing balm,
Heal us with Your touch
Shroud us in Your peace and calm.

Empower us Lord
With Your healing touch,
To mend the wounds of life
That hurt us so much.

Empower us Lord
To acknowledge Your love
So we can live each day
Within Your heavenly touch.

Empower us Lord
In Your enduring love divine,
Like a sweet fragrance
That lingers for all time.

BELIEVE YOUR…
TRUST AND FAITH…

"But he takes pleasure in those who honour him,
in those who trust in his constant love."

Psalm 147 : 11

ARM OF TRUST

No other arm can build
A bridge of security,
When you connect with the Saviour
You will survive reality.

Go out on His arm of trust
When you lose direction in life,
Take that step in faith,
Jesus is your guiding light.

His arm of trust never tires,
He will carry the heaviest load,
When you trip, fall or stumble,
His arms will gather you close.

Go out on His arm of trust
With faith in your heart,
He will never leave you,
He will direct your every path.

A CHILD OF CHRIST

Help me to be
A child of Christ,
You came to me
And showed me your light.

Make me worthy
To be Your child,
To turn from earths ways
To Your heavenly smile.

Help me overcome
The hurdles of life,
To rise above challenges
To Your way in the light.

In You I escape reality
With my faith and trust,
By giving my cares to You
Believing I must.

As a child of Christ
I'm safe in Your arms,
Made in Your image,
I can claim Your peace and calm.

THE PEACE OF GOD

The peace of God is in you
Waiting to be born,
When you respond to His call
Barriers will fall.

You'll turn from your ways
Though challenges will rise,
With the peace of God within you,
You can face the turning tide.

The peace of God is real
When you bow on your knees,
Confessing Him the King of Kings
Who gave you Calvary.

Claim the peace of God,
Walk in His light,
You are His beloved;
And precious in His sight.

JESUS, BE WITH ME

Like the clouds drift on by,
Our days come and go
From one day to the next,
Only God knows.

Keep your faith in the Saviour,
Ask for help today,
"Jesus be with me
Through this day," I pray.

Reality can be harsh
That spoils a peaceful day,
But having the Saviour in my life
Will help to ease the pain.

Turn to His Word for strength,
Be sure His answer will come,
Your troubles will seem lighter,
Left in the Saviour's love.

Jesus, be with me today
As You take my hurts away,
Only through Your mercy and grace
Can I face another day.

HEART MOODS

When heart moods steal the day,
Your focus is in one place,
Look to His light above,
Your sadness He will take.

Claim His help today,
Leave the dark clouds behind,
Your heart can move to sunshine
Where His help abides.

You only need to ask
For the Saviour's loving arms,
Turn to His Word for comfort,
You will find His peace and calm.

Heart moods can change for good
When you surrender to Him,
Confess them all today
So the Holy Spirit's healing can begin.

Give your heart moods to Jesus,
He wants to take them all,
And replace them with His joy
When He receives your call.

EMBRACE ME

Embrace me Dear One
And hold me close,
Quieten my fears
That chill me the most.

Embrace me Dear One
Brighten my life,
Take me to a happy place
Where I can see Your light.

Embrace me Dear One
So I can smile,
Above the challenges
To a life worthwhile.

Embrace me Dear One
In Your warmth divine,
To walk in Your light
That will forever shine.

HIS REVELATION OF LOVE…
BEYOND OUR UNDERSTANDING…

"…What no one ever saw or heard, what no one ever thought could happen, is the very thing God prepared for those who love him."

1 Corinthians 2 : 9

HIGHS AND LOWS

I'm changing course in my life
But I don't know where,
I'm experiencing highs in Your love
And lows in my own despair.

Sometimes I travel mile after mile,
Maintaining the status quo,
Then sometimes in life
I drop to an all time low.

There are times when I need to change
The way I maintain my life,
As long as my heart's in a happy place
The lows will change to highs.

Obedience to the Saviour
Will bring more highs than lows,
But discipline is in order
For my heart to overflow.

THE DAY YOU CAME TO STAY

The day You came to stay Lord,
I will never forget,
I met Your Holy Spirit,
Who gave me heart-rest!

To live within Your arms,
Forever more,
A washing of my spirit
Joined me to Yours.

The day You came to stay,
I saw victory in my life,
I felt Your Holy Spirit
Change the wrong to right.

I never knew pure love
Until that day,
Jesus I'm so glad
The day You came to stay.

I felt a change take place,
My heart was shining bright,
The day You came to stay Lord
Brought a love I just can't hide.

NOURISHMENT

On the days you feel low,
Enthusiasm just can't be found,
Turn to His Word,
Where tender loving care abounds.

It will reinforce His love for you,
Nourishment you will feel,
Set your heart in the right place
To accept what it feels.

Strength will rise to meet you,
His presence will arrive,
Nourishment continues
To help you survive.

On those dim days,
Seek nourishment in Christ,
His love will prevail
If you give Him the time.

TELL ME YOU LOVE ME

Father, Father,
I come as Your child,
Hold me close
For a little while.

Tell me how You love me
And what You see in me,
Any good I can do?
To help someone in need.

Hold me close
In Your loving arms,
Tell me You love me,
Shroud me in Your peace and calm.

I need Your love right now,
Hold me close to Your breast,
So I can forget my loneliness,
I come to You for rest.

LOVING YOU

In loving You Lord
We are set free,
Though the binds of life
Can bring us to our knees.

In times of trial
We must keep our faith,
In loving you
The steps of life we can take.

In love we must
Exalt Your Holy name,
To come before You Father
So we can be changed.

In loving You
We become Your Holy child,
Change our thoughts and ways
To be worthy of Your smile.

HEAL THE HURT

Precious Holy Father
Only You can erase
The pain and shame I feel
When I look into Your face.

Daily life can bring
A torrent of hurt,
But in You I can rise above it
From the lessons I have learnt.

Life isn't easy,
Each horizon a long way off,
Take each hurt to the Saviour,
His care never stops.

The Saviour can heal the hurt
That living brings,
Ask for His healing balm,
He will gather you under His wings.

THE LORD'S LOVE IS…
UNCONDITIONAL…

"Lord, I know you will never stop being merciful to me.
Your love and loyalty will always keep me safe."

Psalm 40 : 11

FLOW OF LIFE

Sometimes life is a struggle
To maintain the status quo,
But keeping our eyes on Jesus
Is reassurance we will know.

Keeping calm and peace
In the flow of life
Brings its challenges,
But with Jesus we will survive.

He is the "Light of the World",
Our great Counsellor and Prince of Peace,
Look to Him for comfort,
You will surely receive.

So when life is a struggle
Or you have joy to share,
Converse with the Saviour
He wants to be with you there.

INVIGORATE ME

Dispel my fears and doubts Lord
So refreshed I can feel,
On those lonely days
When my sorrow seems so real.

Invigorate my heart Lord
To beat with intent,
To feel happy and calm
Despite the loneliness I sense.

Invigorate me Lord
With Your power divine,
As I reach for Your Word
I feel better all the time.

Invigorate me Lord
To invite Your Spirit to live
Forever in my heart,
Your love, He truly is.

SPIRIT TOUCH

His Spirit touch so quiet,
Arrives silently to heal,
A gift so overwhelming,
It makes me want to kneel.

He is the great Comforter
To soothe our hurting hearts,
Lord You gave Him to us
To share our daily path.

His Spirit touch so bright
Like a flame inside,
Moves the heart and soul,
Joy you just can't hide.

Spirit touch a wonder
No words can explain,
A torch inside to cleanse you,
You will never be the same.

COMMUNE WITH THE SAVIOUR

Commune with the Saviour,
Make room in your heart,
He will change you forever
You will walk a different path.

Commune with the Saviour,
He will show you victory,
Though shadows cross your path
He will supply the strength you need.

Commune with the Saviour,
Follow His footsteps of life,
He has gone before you
An ever shining light.

Commune with the Saviour,
You will have Eternity,
To live in His presence
Will be pure rhapsody.

SURGE AHEAD

Surge ahead in the love of God,
Your journey will be fulfilled
With His loving Spirit
That your heart will truly feel.

His Throne of Glory lies waiting
Where your prayers are received,
He holds a Crown of Grace
Exactly for your needs.

Surge ahead in His wisdom
That will last all your days,
He will shield and protect you
As you find your way.

Surge ahead in His power
That is yours for evermore,
Believe in your faith and trust,
He loves you to the core.

Surge ahead in His great love,
Satisfaction through and through,
Be filled with His Spirit,
He truly loves you!

FULL CIRCLE

The Lord can make it right,
Just present the truth
To His Holy Throne,
You know He wants you to.

He loves you full circle,
He just wants you to come,
Whether you're happy or sad
Or whatever you have done.

Just be honest
To the Holy One,
Ask for His forgiveness,
It will surely come.

Confess to the Master,
He will wash you clean inside,
Your heart now renewed
With His love you just can't hide.

He loves you full circle,
He will never change,
Forever and always
He will be the same.

THE GREAT PROVIDER

You are the great provider Lord
For my heart, mind and soul,
I can go to You for everything
For You have made me whole.

You are the great provider,
My heart tells me so,
You are my joy and strength,
That I know.

You are my great provider,
I received Your grace and truth,
Forever within me,
Every day I share with You.

You are my great provider Lord,
My Saviour and my friend,
We will always be together,
In Your world without end.

THE HEART OF GOD

His Spirit will live inside you,
He will prompt you to do your best,
His love surrounds your being,
While in His arms you rest.

Having the heart of God,
No man can ever own,
Until he receives Eternity,
The greatest gift you'll ever know!

Having the heart of God
Knows true, divine love,
Nothing on this earth
Can match the nature of God.

Having the heart of God
Means going the extra mile,
Being caring and kind
To make each day worthwhile.

Having the heart of God
Is to cast your cares,
To step out in faith
And believe He will answer your prayers.

The heart of God
Knows true humility,
In Him all things are possible,
You will rise to victory.

SOME DAYS

Some days Lord, I feel lost,
But one thing I know,
I'll always be in Your love
Because You love me so.

Somedays I lose direction,
My commitment is low,
Distractions in the world
Affect me so.

I have to come back
To Your Holy Word,
It sustains and refreshes me
Where Your love is reaffirmed.

Some days are weary days
But in You I find strength,
Your power and Your glory
Will never ever end.

My faith tells me
I can rise above these days,
In Your sheltered arms
I am carried always.

MY GUIDE

Forgive me for my weakness Lord
And my selfishness too,
Some days it's all about me
But I need to focus on You.

Humanity can be so reckless,
Pride and greed stand in our way,
But if we look to You Lord,
Our heart will surely change.

To know You as my Saviour,
The guide of my life,
Kindness and compassion meet me
Through Your shining light.

Meeting You every day Lord
Will charge the light in me,
Having You as my Saviour
Is all I truly need.

COMMUNE CLOSELY

Commune closely to Jesus,
How sweet that time can be,
Open your soul to Him,
He loves you so tenderly.

Commune closely to Jesus,
Your whispers He will hear,
He loves you so completely,
His Spirit brings Him near.

Commune closely to Jesus,
Tell Him your every thought,
Praise Him to the fullest,
Your freedom He truly bought.

Commune closely to Jesus,
Give Him those doubts inside,
Pass them over to Him,
In you He will abide.

FAITH BRINGS ETERNITY

A tiny step in faith
Is a leap into Eternity,
What joy you will know
When the Saviour; you believe.

Your lessons will be many
But your strength is supplied,
Jesus will never leave you
Because He is your guide.

Faith brings Eternity,
The Saviour's home for you,
Confess He is your "King of Kings"
Is all you have to do!

Little steps each day
Is all you need,
Your faith brings Eternity,
Jesus's face you will see.

PART THREE

"…for God has poured out his love into our hearts
by means of the Holy Spirit, who is God's gift to us."

Romans 5 : 5

THE HOLY SPIRIT …
BRINGS GOD'S LOVE…

"Your constant love is my guide;
Your faithfulness always leads me."

Psalm 26 : 3

FOREVER YOU WILL REIGN

Forever You will reign,
Glorious Lord above,
You will never change,
Mankind is Your true love.

Mankind will always be,
No matter how long the age,
All in Your appointed time,
Forever You will reign.

Years may come and go,
Mankind will as well,
Forever You will reign,
Our story one day we'll tell.

You, the Almighty Father
Sit upon Your Throne,
Forever You will reign,
Where You've made our home.

YOUR LOVE DIVINE

Your love divine pleases my soul,
Untold joy filters through,
I'm walking in Your love today
Because I want to.

Your love divine is so special,
My faith grows at Your touch,
It's Your grace and mercy that feeds me,
I love You so very much.

Your love divine is real,
Devotion time I need every day,
That's when I connect with You,
I feel blessed in so many ways.

Your love divine is so pure,
Nothing on earth can compare,
My heart opens to receive You,
You will live with me there.

ETERNAL SHEPHERD

My Eternal Shepherd
My path in life You see,
Keep me safe in life's journey
Where You watch over me.

Your loving gaze never leaves me,
Whether my path follows creeks and hills,
You never abandon me
My eternal shield.

My path may be narrow
And windy with deep ravines,
But my Shepherd You truly are
Because You are always with me.

My feet You anoint with oil
The sweetest to be found,
My Shepherd I'll love You forever,
My soul is Heaven bound.

ETERNAL TREASURE

Jesus' eternal light
Will shine forever more,
His shores will sparkle and shine,
No one will stumble or fall.

No disputes will be heard,
Jealousy and greed banished forever,
We will love one another
In His eternal treasure.

Harsh words will be silent,
Rules and appointments won't exist,
Peace and calm will reign
At Jesus' home – only perfect bliss.

The rivers of tears dried up,
No broken hearts to be seen,
His pure love, grace and mercy
Are all you'll ever need.

His promise to make things new again
Will surely be fulfilled,
At His home in Glory,
All these things will be revealed.

BELIEVE TO RECEIVE

Believe to receive
In Jesus Christ our Lord,
He loves us so much
It's you He adores.

Believe to receive
Eternal life forever more,
He came to earth so we could live
With Him in one accord.

Believe to receive
His gift of the Holy Spirit,
Who will come to reside
Inside your heart, you will feel Him.

An overwhelming baptism
Of holy, pure love,
Will fill your heart forever
Bringing God's peace and calm.

Your cares He will resolve
When you use your trust and faith,
So believe to receive,
You will know His mercy and grace.

CONNECT AS ONE

The Lord's channel is always open,
Like the rays of the sun
Reaching down to earth,
Connecting as one.

Nothing can stop His connection with us
Because of His great love,
He made us in His image,
So we can live as one.

The choice is ours
When the Holy Spirit speaks,
To accept His love completely
Will take you to His Holy Seat.

Forgiven by His grace,
We can connect as one,
Take hold of His Holy Spirit,
He will show you the Son.

Connect to His channel
Through His golden rays
Which will fill you to overflow,
His life for you He gave.

THE SWEET FRAGRANCE…
OF HIS GREAT LOVE…

"We love because God first loved us."

1 John 4 : 19

HIS GIFT OF LOVE

His gift of love so special
To every believing heart,
Can only come from God,
From you He will never depart.

His gift of love so pure
Nothing on earth can compare,
Receive this gift from the Saviour,
His robe of grace you will wear.

His gift of love for mankind
Is free for every soul,
Confess with your lips "He is Lord",
You will receive blessings untold.

Yes, blessings to you will flow
Beyond your belief,
Compassion and kindness you'll know,
To believe is to receive.

SOLITUDE

In solitude we find peace,
Calmer thoughts can reside,
Make this your time with Jesus
To repair any hurts inside.

Solitude demands discipline
For this heart of mine,
It's catch-up time with the Saviour
To reflect and pass the time.

The Lord had to find solitude,
He went to the mountains to pray,
To be close to His Father,
Peace and calm He craved.

We all need those moments
To be calm and still,
To revive the heart and soul
And meditate on His will.

So for healing and peace,
Seek solitude with the Lord,
Heal yourself and move forward,
Great will be your reward!

WE ARE LOVED

We are loved by the Lord Almighty
No matter what we think,
Who we are or where we live,
We are still His child to Him.

He made us in His image,
He gave us a heart and soul,
He's prepared a heavenly home,
For each of His fold.

He calls us all "beloved",
He loves us unconditionally,
He bore our sins at Calvary
So we can be free of iniquity.

He gave us the Holy Spirit,
To reveal Himself to us,
A bounty of wonder and glory
Is ours when we accept His love.

Open your heart to the Saviour,
You will have eternal life,
To live forever in His kingdom,
Where He is the shining light.

I'M IN YOUR LOVING HANDS

I'm in Your loving hands Lord,
My course in life unknown,
But I must look to You
For the seeds I need to sow.

I'm gripped by Your Grace
So divinely given by You,
So I look for Your direction
That will guide me through.

You placed in me
Your divine endowment of love,
Because I am saved
Your Spirit will show me "The Son".

I'm in Your loving hands Lord,
Your precious Spirit tells me so,
He comforts and guides me,
That I surely know.

PEACE AND CALM

In peace and calm
I come to You,
Loving You Lord
And needing You too.

You are my strength
No matter what,
When I focus on You
My fears will stop.

In trust and faith
I claim Your help,
To Your divine love
I can help myself.

In Your peace and calm
I can have victory,
Every day of my life
I have to come to Thee.

NURTURE ME

Free me in Your grace
That nurtures me,
Every day of my life
You set me free.

Your everlasting love
That powers me on,
Nothing can bind me down
Because to You I belong.

Your arms will hold me
Firm and safe,
Nurture me with Your Spirit,
He shows me Your face.

You feed me so my faith will grow
Without me even knowing,
Nurture me in Your love
So I can see where I am going.

PART FOUR

"But because of our sins he was wounded, beaten
because of the evil we did. We are healed by the
punishment he suffered, made whole by the
blows he received."

Isaiah 53 : 5

THEIR LAST MEAL TOGETHER…
THE SACRED EUCHARIST…

"Jesus sent Peter and John with these instructions:"
"Go and get the Passover meal ready for us to eat."
"He will show you a large furnished room upstairs,
where you will get everything ready."

Luke 22 : 8, 12

THE UPPER ROOM

The Lord Himself
And His chosen few,
Shared a meal
In the Upper Room.

The Upper Room so sacred,
So profound in many ways
Of eating together and singing hymns,
But His Father; He will obey.

His Disciples couldn't know
The trauma so near,
Of the pain to come
And how they would scatter in fear.

It would be their last time together
Eating the Bread and sharing the Wine,
To remember Him forever,
A Sacrament, so divine.

His heart breaking
For the betrayal so near,
For a pouch full of silver
To name the One so Dear.

Once more we will share
The Bread and the Wine,
When He returns in great glory
To receive His waiting Bride.

MURMURS OF EASTER

The murmurs of Easter
Call the soul,
Eternal love calling
From a heart of pure gold.

Emotion is raw,
His power reigns,
A sacrifice given
In magnified pain.

A load so heavy
Borne only by God,
Sent for the many
From a promise that was.

The murmurs of Easter
Stir the soul,
Down through the ages
His story unfolds.

His power and glory
Forever will reign,
Because of God's Son
We will never be the same.

BLESSED ONE, CHRIST JESUS

Blessed One, Christ Jesus,
King of Kings and Lord of Lords,
My Holy Saviour,
We are one accord.

You carried Your Cross to Calvary,
The pinnacle of Your life on earth,
Raised up before the world,
Your mission was to serve.

Words just can't explain
The emotion inside,
When I think of the Saviour
For mankind crucified.

Nothing would have stopped Him,
Giving His life for us,
As revealed in the Holy Scriptures,
He drank His Father's Cup.

Victory was His,
God raised Him from the grave,
Blessed One, Christ Jesus
Lives for us today!

SPLENDOUR IN THE GARDEN …
THE SAVIOUR IS ALIVE…

"Woman, why are you crying?" Jesus asked her.
"Who is it that you are looking for?"
"She thought he was the gardener, so she said to him,
"If you took him away, sir, tell me where you have
put him, and I will go and get him."
Jesus said to her, "Mary! ..."

John 20 : 15, 16

I REJOICE

I rejoice Dear One,
Your Father raised You to life,
Your body and blood were given
That gave us eternal life.

I rejoice Dear One
In glorious You,
Your precious Holy Spirit,
A gift to help us through.

I rejoice in You Lord
Now risen from the Grave,
You live, You live, You live,
You live for me today.

Thank You Dear One
For all You do for us,
I'm so glad You live today
To build a Kingdom for us.

No stone could hold You captive,
No tomb too dark or cold,
Grave clothes now scattered,
You wear a Robe of Gold!

HE LIVES

Surround yourself in beauty,
Be touched by joy divine,
Behold His glorious presence,
He lives; God divine.

Feel deep His Spirit within
That brings His Holy love,
Let it nurture and bless you,
You will know His peace from above.

When you share His Communion Cup,
It symbolizes His blood shed for you,
Your sins forgiven from that moment on,
Remember His love that is pure.

This drove Him to Calvary,
He bore your sins to set you free,
The one true vine forever,
He lives for you and me.

WONDER AND AWE...
THE ARRIVAL OF THE SAVIOUR...

"This very day in David's town your Saviour was born-Christ the Lord!" "And this is what will prove it to you: you will find a baby wrapped in cloths and lying in a manger."

Luke 2 : 11, 12

A DIMLY LIT STABLE

Joseph took care of Mary
As they travelled to Bethlehem,
Through the cold winter nights
On their way to the Inn.

In the dimly lit stable
Mary gave birth,
She wrapped Him snuggly,
He was her very first.

In the dimly lit stable
The shepherds arrived,
And the Magi with gifts
In the awe of the night.

The sheep and the cattle
Followed them too,
They came to worship Him,
The Saviour they knew.

As they adored Him,
God's glory revealed,
On that Holiest of nights
Our redemption was sealed!

IN THE SILENCE OF THE NIGHT

In the silence of the night
Heavenly angels came forth,
They sang with great joy
The birth of the Lord.

In awe and in wonder
The shepherds came to see
And worship the Baby Messiah
That led them to believe.

Mary and Joseph overwhelmed
By the arrival of the Lord,
As prophesied in His Word
Many centuries before.

In the silence of the night
The Magi came to adore,
With gifts from the East
For the newborn; Lord of Lords!

The silence of the night
Gave way to this heavenly sight,
The arrival of Baby Jesus
On that Holiest of nights.

THE NEWBORN MESSIAH KING

In the quiet of the night,
The Bethlehem Babe was born,
The Star high above
Shone down glory until the dawn.

What wonder and awe revealed
On that Holy night,
The Saviour in the Manger
Adored by the shepherds that night.

Three Kings from the East
Arrived with precious gifts,
Bowed lowly before Him
The newborn Messiah King.

The sheep and the cattle layed down
As they looked upon the Holy Christ,
They knew He was their maker
On that heavenly Holy night.

The newborn Messiah King;
Glorious in every way,
Came to be our Saviour
In Bethlehem that very day!

HOLY LOVE

Under the Star of David,
His Holy love began,
From that moment He was born,
He was crowned the "Son of Man".

His Holy love will shroud you
Wherever you are in the world,
To every heart that knows Him,
He will reveal Himself.

His Holy love so pure,
Comes from the Lord Himself,
To every heart that believes,
He came to save the world.

Yes, Holy love was born
Centuries ago,
The Messiah came to save us
Because He loves us so!

Holy love can only be
From the Sovereign God Himself,
Through the Three in One; The Trinity
Holy love will reveal itself!

ALSO BY CLAIRE GROSE

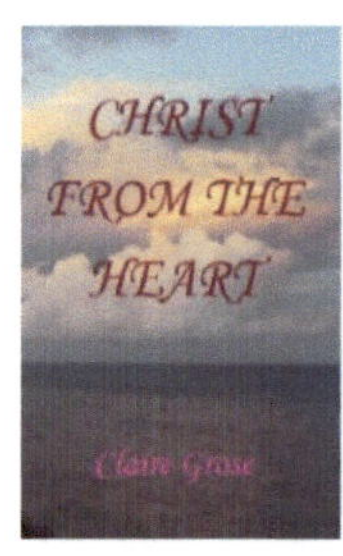

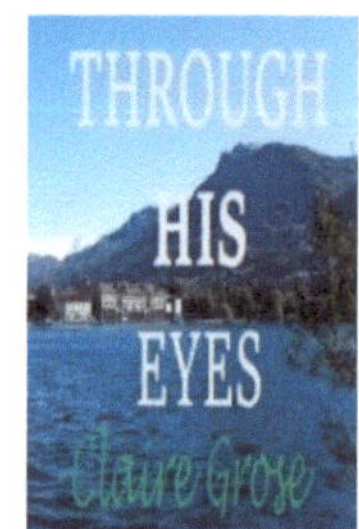

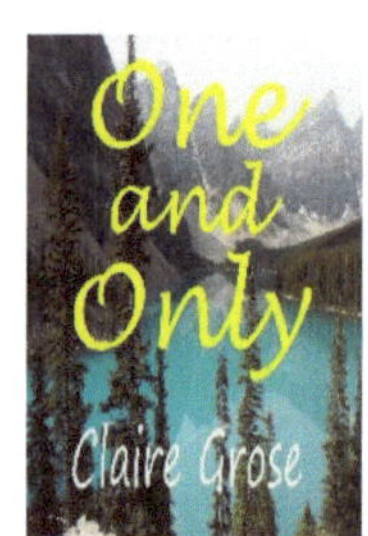

ABOUT THE AUTHOR

Claire worked as a Government Public Servant in the Lands Department, Adelaide, South Australia until she married and became a mother of two boys.

She later returned to the work force during which time she gained a "Living Hope" Phone Counselling certificate which influenced her need to help others.

Through this and personal experience she found herself inspired by God's love to put pen to paper.

PHOTO CREDITS

COVER PHOTO: Flowering Lavender – photo taken by Claire Grose

Page 2: Pink Camelia; Victoria – Jeanette and Pete
Page 12: Guinea Fowls; N.S.W. - Allan and Barry
Page 24: Peace Rose; S.A. – Claire Grose
Page 31: "Night Sky" Miniature Petunias; S.A. – Claire Grose
Page 39: Cordyline; Queensland – Carol and Den
Page 47: Lavender; S.A. – Claire Grose
Page 55: Pink Blossom: Tanunda, S.A. – Claire Grose
Page 70: Foreshore Rocks; Hastings Point, N.S.W. – Claire Grose
Page 78: Flowering Jacaranda; Pt. Vincent, S.A. – Claire Grose
Page 87: Angaston Vines; S.A. – Claire Grose
Page 92: Pink Rose; Veale Gardens, S.A. – Claire Grose
Page 96: Red Camelia; Victoria. – Jeanette and Pete

www.ingramcontent.com/pod-product-compliance
Lightning Source LLC
Chambersburg PA
CBHW061030100726
47911CB00001B/28